The Hit and Run GANG 3
THE SLUMP

Don't Miss Any of the
On-the-Field Excitement with
THE HIT AND RUN GANG
by Steven Kroll
from Avon Books

(#1) NEW KID IN TOWN
(#2) PLAYING FAVORITES
(#4) THE STREAK

STEVEN KROLL grew up in New York City, where he was a pretty good first baseman and #3 hitter on baseball teams in Riverside Park. He graduated from Harvard University, spent almost seven years as an editor in book publishing, and then became a full-time writer. He is the author of more than fifty books for young people. He and his wife Abigail live in New York City and root for the Mets.

The Hit and Run GANG 3
THE SLUMP

STEVEN KROLL

Illustrated by Meredith Johnson

AN AVON CAMELOT BOOK

THE HIT AND RUN GANG #3: THE SLUMP is an original publication of Avon Books. This work has never before appeared in book form. This work is a novel. Any similarity to actual persons or events is purely coincidental.

AVON BOOKS
A division of
The Hearst Corporation
1350 Avenue of the Americas
New York, New York 10019

For Elizabeth Levy

Contents

1. Getting Into It

"Stee-rike three!"

The umpire's call echoed through the April afternoon. Lucas Emory, spark-plug catcher of the Raymondtown Rockets baseball team, stood in the batter's box. For a moment, he was too dazed to move.

"Sorry, Luke," said the ump, "it was a strike."

The truth of this finally sank in. Luke stepped out of the box and trudged back to the dugout. He took off his helmet and collapsed on the bench.

He'd just let his best pitch go by. It was a fastball down and away. Usually he liked to step into that pitch and pound it to the opposite field. But not this time, and not in practice this past week. Not in yesterday's game against the Barons, which the Rockets eventually won when Jenny Carr stole home in the bottom of the sixth inning. And not in any at bat earlier today either.

It was the top of the fifth in the Rockets' first away game of the season. They were playing the Pelicans in Healesville, and in his first two at bats, Luke had grounded out to short and foul tipped a third strike into Lane Rudolph's, the opposing catcher's, mitt. He couldn't seem to stop messing up, and he was definitely not going to get another chance this afternoon!

The Rockets were far behind, 7–2, and they seemed flat. Andy McClellan had arrived for practice sick to his stomach, so Josh Rubin got the start. But Josh had turned out to be really wild. He'd walked too many with that odd sidearm delivery of his, and then he'd given up a few big hits. On top of that, the kids were really nervous playing on a lumpy field they had never seen before and in front of a bunch of hothead home-team fans. They made some costly errors. By the time Brian Krause replaced Josh in the bottom of the third and Josh took over Brian's spot at short, the damage was done.

The Rockets hadn't scored since the second inning when big Pete Wyshansky came rumbling in from third on Michael Wong's checked-swing base hit to right. Now, because of Luke, there were two out in the fifth. Not many chances left.

Luke watched grimly as Phil Hubbard, the Rockets' third baseman, worked the count to three and two. The Pelican pitcher wasn't fast, but he seemed to be able to throw a strike whenever he really needed one. He wound and threw, and Phil stroked a single into left center field!

Luke was on his feet, along with everyone else on the Rockets' bench. "Go, Phil!" he shouted, but the throw came in to second and Phil had to stop at first.

He took a two step lead as Brian Krause let the first pitch go by for a strike. Even so late in the game, this guy was challenging the hitters, but Brian wasn't intimidated. He just crouched a little lower, took a few practice swings, and belted the next pitch, a big fat change-up, into the left field corner.

With two out, Phil was running on the pitch. He tore around second and kept on going. As he roared into third, the left fielder was still getting the ball out of his glove. Coach Carr windmilled him home, and Phil made the turn and scored standing up as the ball got only as far as the shortstop cut-off man.

Justin Carr, the on-deck hitter, was there to give Phil a high-five, but Luke was right behind him.

"Good going, kid!" he shouted, their hands slapping together. "We can do it now!"

The Pelicans were ahead, 7–3, but it looked as if Luke might be right. Brian was dancing around out on second base, and the devoted group of Raymondtown fans, who had come all the way to Healesville to support their team, finally had something to cheer about.

"Rah Rah Rockets!" they shouted. *"Rah Rah Rockets!"*

The air was filled with electricity. Justin singled to right, scoring Brian all the way from second. Pete Wyshansky worked the count to 2 and 0, then got his pitch and homered to straightaway center. Racing around the bases instead of doing a home run trot, he crossed the plate right behind Justin and stamped on it. 7–6 Pelicans and not done yet!

The Pelicans brought in a new pitcher, a big, heavyset right-hander named Herb Kelly. Even after warming up, Kelly seemed uncomfortable. Either he hadn't pitched very much in the past or he wasn't accustomed to coming in under this kind of pressure.

Immediately Jenny Carr tagged him for a broken bat single down the third base line and took second when the left fielder bobbled the ball. Giving up the extra base seemed to fluster Kelly even more. He threw a wild pitch to Michael Wong, and Jenny scampered down to third. He walked Michael on four pitches, then little Vicky Lopez stepped in, took a ball and a strike, and smacked a bouncer over the second baseman's head

5

that scored Jenny and sent Michael over to third.

Unfortunately Josh Rubin flied out to end the threat, but with the Rockets taking the field for the bottom half of the fifth, the score was tied at 7!

Luke was overjoyed. Any thoughts of striking out were gone from his head. As he strapped on his catcher's gear, all he could think was: We can win it—and *I'm* leading off in the sixth!

Brian was cruising now. He struck out the first batter on three pitches, then coaxed a little infield nubbler out of the second. But he started getting overconfident, walked the next batter, then gave up a double to right that moved the runner on first over to third.

Luke was out to the mound in a moment, settling down his pitcher. "Come on, Brian," he said. "We can win this game. Just throw strikes."

Brian nodded, but he wasn't throwing strikes. Second and third with two out had him thinking too hard and overthrowing. Ball 1. Ball 2. And then—a line drive over Josh Rubin's head, Jenny running hard from left, the runner coming down the line from third, there was going to be a play at the plate!

Luke crouched low, got ready. Jenny's throw was right on the money. The runner slid in hard, but as the dust rose and Luke felt himself going over, he made the tag.

"Out!" yelled the umpire, and there was barrel-chested Luke, sprawled in the dirt, the ball still in his hand, the runner still out.

He sprang up, waving the ball over his head. Phil hugged him, and so did half the team. The Rockets came to bat with the score still tied 7–7.

The hometown crowd had been cheering hard for their Pelicans. Now they grew quiet as Luke stepped into the batter's box, anchored his back foot, and took a few swings.

"Hit it out!" shouted Jordan Smithers, one of the Rockets' substitutes.

Luke took a breath and let it go. He faced Herb Kelly, concentrated as hard as he could, watched the P on Kelly's cap, waited for the ball to come over the

top. He'd saved the game for the Rockets, and now they were going to win it.

Kelly didn't seem uncomfortable anymore. The half inning's rest had made the difference. He reared and fired a fastball up and in. Luke took it, and the umpire yelled "Stee-rike one!"

Luke stepped out of the box, rubbed his hands in the dirt, swung the bat once, stepped back in. Come on, Kelly, he thought, give me a pitch to hit.

And Kelly did. He wound and fired another fastball, but this one was right down the middle of the plate.

Luke took a tremendous cut. He swung so hard he practically fell down. What he wanted to see was the ball leap off his bat, heading for left field and extra bases. What he saw was a cute little pop-up that the shortstop squeezed for the out.

2. Quiet Time

Luke was so mad, he could taste it. He pounded his bat on the plate and once again trudged back to the Rockets' dugout.

Having grown so quiet before, the Pelican fans were going wild now. Their cheers and shouts followed Luke all the way to the bench and kept on coming as he pulled off his helmet and flung it on the ground.

Coach Channing came right over. "All right, Luke, that's enough, you know you don't win games that way." He put his arm around him. They sat down together.

Luke tried to keep the tears from squeezing out of the corners of his eyes. He knew he'd been dressed down for throwing his helmet, but he wanted to tell the coach that you don't win games, especially when they're tie games, by leading off in the top of the sixth and popping up either. He wanted to say that he just knew that because of him the team had somehow lost its momentum, and because of him they could lose a game they probably should have won.

And he was right. Phil Hubbard got up and bounced out to Kelly on the mound. Brian Krause followed, worked the count to 3 and 1, and lofted a soft fly ball directly at the center fielder. The Rockets were flat again. They went quietly, one-two-three, and the score was still tied 7–7 going into the bottom of the sixth.

And then the bottom fell out. Brian got the first Pelican batter on a high foul that Justin Carr reached up and caught two steps from the bag at first, but then Kelly came up and promptly lined a double over Justin's head. This got Brian rattled, and his next pitch, to a big girl pinch hitter named Dixie Rothwell, was wild. Luke tried to knock it down, but it caromed all the way to the backstop and Kelly made it over to third easily. With that, Brian served one up to Dixie. She looped a single over Vicky Lopez's head at second, Kelly came in to score, and the game was over.

It was Kelly who had done it to Luke on his last at bat and Kelly who was now dancing on the plate as his teammates gathered round. Luke stayed in his crouch for a moment, then took off his mask and walked away. He'd been right about everything, but it didn't make him feel good. He was the one who hadn't come through when the others had. He was the one who'd lost them their momentum and made them lose the game.

The two teams lined up to shake hands at home plate. Luke tried to be sincere in his handshakes, but it was pretty hard, particularly when it came to Kelly. Phil and Brian came over to talk to him afterwards, but he was feeling too lousy to talk to anyone. He helped gather up all the gear, then sat on the bench by himself as everyone else got ready to leave.

He was still there, looking at the ground, when someone behind him started chanting.

The chant was very low, almost a whisper, and at first Luke couldn't make it out. He listened hard, and it got clearer.

"Slump, slump, slump," he heard. "Slump, slump, slump."

He whirled around, and there stood Pete Wyshansky, leaning against a bat, grinning.

"You're really into it, aren't you?" Pete said. "Think you'll get another hit this season?"

Luke stood up, hands on hips. "I am *not* in a slump," he said, "and you've got some nerve telling me that I am!"

"Touchy, touchy."

"I'll touchy-touchy you! Get out of here and leave me alone, Pete!"

Pete tipped his cap and was gone. Luke returned to the bench. Was Pete right? Could he be in a slump? He'd never even considered it. Not him. Not Luke Emory. But could he be?

He heard a car horn, three short

blasts, and there were Phil and Brian back again, the light glinting off Brian's glasses, wisps of blond hair sticking out from under Phil's baseball cap.

"Come on, Luke," Phil said. "Dad's ready."

Oh, yes, Luke remembered now. Phil's dad was driving the three of them home. "Sorry," he said, and followed his friends to the parking lot.

The ride home was filled with quiet. Sitting in back behind Mr. Hubbard, Luke was glad of that. Everyone looked straight ahead at the road as the daylight began to fade. Quiet time. Quiet time was what he needed.

As they reached Raymondtown, Phil said from the front seat, "It wasn't your fault, Luke."

The statement hung in the gloom. Then Luke said, unconvincingly, "I know."

"I screwed up pitching, and I screwed up hitting," Brian said. "If losing was anyone's fault, it was mine."

This was what he wished they wouldn't do. Nothing they could say would make

15

him feel better or give him any excuse. He was supposed to be the leader. He wasn't supposed to screw up in the clutch.

"Thanks, guys," Luke said. "I'll be all right."

"Why don't we stop for some pizza?" Phil's father suggested. "One slice apiece won't spoil your dinners."

"Yeah," said Phil, "pizza."

"Hey, great!" said Brian.

"Thanks, Mr. Hubbard," said Luke, "but I think I'll pass. Too much homework."

"Okay, Luke," said Phil's dad. "I'll drop you off first."

A few minutes later the familiar driveway appeared. Luke said his good-byes and opened the back door of the Volvo.

"See you at school," Phil said.

"Yuh, see you," Luke said.

Quiet time, he thought as he went up the stairs to his house. Quiet time, he thought as the front door burst open and his little brother Jamey grabbed his legs and shouted, "Did you win, Lukey?"

The events of the afternoon welled up in him, and with them came the anger. "Is that how you say 'hello', Jamey?" he shouted back. "Is that all you care about?"

He slammed his catcher's mitt on the floor and stormed to his room.

Ten minutes went by, and there was a knock on the door.

"Come in," Luke said.

It was his father, an older version of himself. He shut the door and sat on the bed.

"You must have had a bad day."

Luke nodded.

"I saw it on your face when you walked in, but Jamey's too little to have seen that, Luke. He was just glad to have his big brother home. Do you understand that?"

"Yes," said Luke, "I'll apologize. I just got mad. I didn't mean to hurt Jamey."

His father smiled. "I'm glad to hear that, but there's something else."

"What?"

"It's okay to lose. Losing will make you tougher tomorrow. But I have the

17

feeling there was more today. Am I right?"

His father knew something was going on. He hadn't been at the game today because he'd had to work, but he knew anyway. His father had taught him everything about baseball. Because of his father, he'd been able to coach Phil Hubbard enough to help him make the Rockets. He couldn't admit to his father he'd failed. It made him feel too bad.

"No," Luke said. "Everything's cool."

"Okay. Let's have dinner."

3. Paying Attention

At the dinner table, Luke sat next to Jamey and messed up his hair. "I'm sorry I was mean, Jamey," he said. "The Rockets lost today and I was upset."

There was a pause. Then Jamey said, "That's okay, Lukey."

What a relief. Luke turned his attention to being cheerful with his parents. He talked up school and the Rockets and how nice Mr. Hubbard was to drive him home from the game. He even ate all his vegetables and a banana dessert he didn't especially like. Then he excused himself and went to his room.

Behind the closed door, he sat at his desk. Was he overhitting? Was he trying too hard? He couldn't figure it out, but these thoughts kept getting in the way of the math problems he was supposed to be doing and the spelling words he was supposed to have memorized for the test tomorrow.

For some ridiculous reason, he kept writing the word "bandanna" as "banana," probably in honor of that messy dessert he'd just eaten and didn't like. Finally, in desperation, he looked over at the poster of Roy Campanella, the great Brooklyn Dodger catcher of the 1950s, he had hanging on his door. Luke's father had seen Campanella play and had told him how terrific he was.

Campanella was smiling. Crouched behind the plate, his arm cocked to throw, all he seemed to be saying was "Nail another man at second."

The next morning, Luke's dad dropped him off at school in the ancient blue Buick. Would someone get to him about his bad game? Would Pete Wyshansky taunt him about the slump he wasn't in?

He strode through the door, short and stocky, fists clenched, ready for the worst. A red-haired kid called Bert passed him in the hall and said "Tough luck about the loss, Luke." There was a hush when he walked into Mrs. Irvington's room, but it was the same sort of hush that happened whenever someone came in unexpectedly. He passed by Pete Wyshansky's seat on his way to his own, and Pete looked up and said, "Oh, hi, Luke."

Luke tensed himself for more, but somehow, miraculously, that was it.

Then, right away, the spelling test seemed to be happening. Mrs. Irvington passed out sheets of paper and stood in the front of the room reading out the words. Luke's mind dissolved in a haze. Words appeared and disappeared before his eyes. *Bandanna banana bandanna banana.* By the time the test was over, he was sure he had done terribly.

And then, before he could blink, there was math.

He fidgeted in his seat, looked out the window, played with his pencil and the eraser on the end.

21

"Luke," Mrs. Irvington said, "would you please tell us the answer?"

Luke looked up. He hadn't even heard the question.

"I—I don't know."

"Lucas Emory, would you please remember you are in school today and not at a baseball game?"

Luke swallowed hard. "Yes, Mrs. Irvington."

He glanced away.

After math, the class went to play kickball in the gym, and he hated it even more than usual. He got off a couple of good shots, but kicking a great big rubber ball seemed so dumb when you could be drawing a bead on a baseball.

Finally there was lunch. He was sitting alone in a corner of the cafetorium when tall, gangly Jordan Smithers draped himself over a chair and started asking about catching.

Ordinarily Luke would have loved this. He would have gone on and on about the best way to stop a passed ball or whether to throw from a crouch when

22

the runner has a good jump. Today he just mumbled a few things about blocking the plate and sent a puzzled Jordan away.

Phil and Brian were hovering nearby. They'd move a few steps toward him, then stop and look away.

Finally Brian walked right up to him. "Luke," he said, "you've got to talk to us."

"Why?" said Luke. "What about?"

"About your slump. If you're in one, we want to help you get out of it."

Luke banged his fist on the table. "I'm not in a slump! I've had a few bad days, that's all. Can't you guys let me work things out?"

"Luke," said Brian, "I—"

"Enough!"

Luke stormed out of the cafetorium. He didn't stop until he got to the boys' bathroom.

He washed his face and pressed a paper towel against it. He knew his friends only wanted to help, but why were they insisting he was in a slump? He was sure he wasn't. He just had to

get himself together, do a little work on his own.

After school, he went straight home. There was no practice on Monday, and he rummaged around in the garage until he found the old batting tee his father had made for him. It was nothing but a piece of plywood with a length of hose stuck in the middle, but Luke set it up in the backyard, got out a bat and ball, stuck the ball in the top of the tee, and began to hit.

For an hour he whammed that ball off the tee into the backyard fence. Just the way he did when he tried to help other players, he explained to himself that he had to concentrate, keep his eye on the ball, and relax. Of course no pitch was being thrown, but he wasn't doing anything wrong!

When he had finished with the batting tee, he spent another half hour fungoing the ball against the fence. Good for concentration and good for timing. He'd throw the ball up, meet it squarely with the bat, and slam it into the fence.

25

He was even catching the top half, just as he knew he should be doing.

It was getting dark when Luke finished up and went inside. He was sweating and tired in the April chill, but he didn't care. He was hitting the ball well. That was all that mattered.

In the kitchen, his mom was fixing dinner. Little Jamey was snoozing in his stroller. As Luke came through, Mom said, "Working hard?"

"Yes, ma'am."

Mom laughed. "You're just like your father, and a good thing, too."

She put down her wooden spoon and hugged him. She was much taller than he was and had to bend way over, but he loved it and hugged her back.

4. Cold Feet

After dinner, Luke talked baseball with his dad. He still wouldn't mention anything about his hitting, but he felt so good about the afternoon, it didn't make any difference.

They were still talking when the phone rang.

"Luke, it's for you," Mom said.

It was Phil.

"Hey, man, what's happenin'?"

"I probably shouldn't be calling," Phil said, "I just—well—"

"Phil," Luke said, "I know I sort of snapped at you at lunch, and I really appreciate your call, but I don't have a problem."

"Good," Phil said, sounding even more nervous, "I just thought, you were so much help to me, if I could help you—"

Luke began to get angry, felt it bubbling up, but he held it in. "Thanks, Phil, but I don't need any extra practice."

It was true. He was back in charge. He couldn't wait to get through school the next day, couldn't wait to get to practice. The spelling test came back, and he'd gotten half the words wrong, including bandanna. Mrs. Irvington scolded him. He promised to do better, concentrated a little more on math and reading, waited for the bell.

Then, when school let out, he got cold feet. Would he mess up again? Would Wyshansky get on him?

He went home and set up the batting tee. He felt himself caressing the bat, shifting his weight, snapping his wrists as he whacked the ball and followed through. He practiced so long and hard he was very late for practice at the ballfield.

When he got there, tall, black-bearded Coach Channing was working with Andy McClellan on the mound. He excused himself and trotted over.

"So what's the story?"

"I'm sorry I'm late," Luke said.

"Late? You've missed half of practice, *all* of hitting practice. You're supposed to set an example for the other players. Do you have an excuse?"

The part about not setting an example stung Luke the most. He realized he'd been wrong, but he didn't know what to say. "I got delayed," he said.

The coach looked as if he might explode. "You what?" he said, and then he stopped. "Luke, come with me a minute."

They went over to the home team dugout and sat on the bench. "Luke," the coach began, "I know you've missed hitting practice—"

"It's okay," Luke said. "It's cool."

"What I'm trying to say," Coach Channing continued, "is if you're concerned about your hitting—"

"I'm not," Luke said, "I'm fine."

"—you can always stay late and do some work with Coach Lopez."

Luke was touched. "Thank you, sir, but I don't need to do that."

Coach Channing placed his hands on his thighs. "Well, okay, just thought you'd want to know I wasn't blind. Let's get out there now and finish up proud!"

And that's exactly what Luke did. He took over the catcher's gear from Justin Carr and got down to business. He threw out runners going down to second. He got Michael Wong in a hot-box drill between third and home and tagged him out before he could score. He sparked the infield and caught for Andy and Josh and Justin, too.

Afterwards, before anyone could leave, Coach Channing strode to the mound. "I've got an announcement," he said. "Instead of practice tomorrow, we have a game. The Bombers can't play Sunday, so we had to change the schedule. Assuming this doesn't create problems for any of you, please be here in your game uniforms for warmups at three-thirty."

A game tomorrow! Luke was thrilled. He'd have his chance even sooner than he expected.

On the way home, he and Phil stopped at Angelo's Pizza on Market Street for a slice. As they dug in, Phil said, "At least you're getting what you missed the other night."

"Yeah," Luke said, "I was sorry about that. I had to get home."

"You're feeling better now?"

"Yeah. That game, it just really got to me."

"Think you'll break out of your slump tomorrow?"

There it was again. *Slump, slump, slump*. Why did it keep coming up? He'd done the necessary work. He was fine.

"Would you please get off my case, Phil?" Luke said. "I'll be ready for the game. You'll see."

"You missed hitting practice this afternoon."

"Who are you, my mother? I did some practicing at home. It got late—"

"Don't get upset, Luke. We need you. We want you to get back on track."

"I am on track. Don't worry so much. Don't worry at all."

"Okay. I'll try."

Phil swallowed hard and took another bite of pizza. "What do you think of Pelsky?"

Fred Pelsky was the likely starting pitcher for the Bombers. Neither Phil nor Luke had ever faced him, but Luke had heard the reports.

"He throws a lot of junk. Bet he'll be tough."

"We'll have our work cut out for us," Phil said.

Our work cut out for us, Luke thought, bounding out of bed the next morning. He'd sailed through his homework last night. He was going out there today and doing it!

He felt so good that before he left for school, he took Jamey out in the backyard for a game of catch. He put his dad's glove on his little brother's hand and tossed him the ball.

"Catch, Jamey," he said.

Jamey stood there teetering. The glove on his hand looked bigger than he was. "Catch," he said, and dropped the ball.

Luke tried again. "Catch, Jamey."

"Catch," said Jamey as the ball hit the ground.

Luke tried a few more times with the same result. Finally he said, "Well, maybe not just yet, Jamey," and took him inside. But he felt good about having made the effort. That was the important thing, until he was about to leave and Jamey said, "Win, Lukey."

Ever the motormouth, Luke was speechless. "Sure, man," he said, poking him in the ribs. Then he got out the door.

5. The Ostrich League

Nothing was going to get to him today! He breezed through his classes, knew every answer on the math quiz, even ate a good lunch. Then he got his uniform on and was the first one at the ballfield.

He always liked being there by himself. Sometimes he went at dusk, when no one else was around, just to be there. He liked standing on second base and feeling at the center of the world.

"Luke?"

It was Andy McClellan, who would be the starting pitcher for the Rockets this afternoon. Andy towered over Luke and was always pushing that shock of black hair out of his eyes.

"Hi, Andy. This place get to you, too?"

"Yeah. Can we talk about the game?"

"Sure."

They sat in the dugout and talked about what pitches Andy was going to throw and when Luke would use signs and how they would handle the runners. By the time they were through, the others had arrived, and it was time for stretches and calisthenics and pre-game practice.

Just like at yesterday's practice, Luke was a demon behind the plate. He fired down to second. He scooped up throws from short and third. He kept the team hustling. And when it was his turn to hit, he stepped in confidently. Coach Carr was pitching down the middle with good speed. Luke smacked the first pitch right at Brian at short. He dumped a couple of ground balls, then got off a good shot to left. Not terrific but improving. He buckled on his catcher's gear so he could warm up Andy.

There wasn't a big crowd—mid-week, everyone's parents at work, unexpected game—but Luke could feel the drama happening as he settled down behind the plate and the first Bomber hitter stepped in.

Andy came out smoking. He struck out that first batter and the second one, too. The third grounded out weakly back to the box. As the Rockets trotted in from the field, Luke got ready to face Fred Pelsky.

He took a few practice swings. Then he took a few more with the doughnut. Then he stepped into the batter's box, ground in his back heel, got his arms back, his head down. Watch what Pelsky throws!

Pelsky had a big windup with a high kick. Luke tried not to be distracted by that. He watched the ball, and in it came, a big, slow change. It looked so ripe, you could belt it a mile. Luke took a big cut and missed. He was so surprised he hadn't put the ball in center field, he couldn't quite believe it.

He stepped out and stepped in again. The next pitch was a fastball up and in, another kind of surprise since Pelsky

wasn't supposed to have a fastball. Luke took it for a strike, and he was down 0 and 2.

Don't panic here. Stand your ground. Make contact. Luke was all concentration as Pelsky wound and fired—way outside. Ball 1. What would be next? Would he challenge? Would he go for the corners?

In it came, a fat, looping change. Luke swung! The ball caromed off the handle of his bat and landed in front of the plate. He was so bewildered, he couldn't move. The Bomber catcher tagged him out before he could even start toward first base.

Luke stormed to the bench and sat down. He was furious, speechless, overwhelmed.

Coach Channing shook him by the shoulder. "Luke," he said, "you've got to stop this. Try and relax. You're way out in front."

How many times had Luke said things like that to others? He folded his arms, looked at the ground, and nodded grimly, just as Phil Hubbard struck out and flopped on the bench beside him.

"Hey, Luke," Phil whispered, "want to join the Ostrich League?"

"The what?"

"The Ostrich League. We could bury our heads in the sand."

Luke snorted and slapped Phil on the shoulder, but just then Andy hit a clean shot over third for a single. "Hey!" Luke shouted, and he and Phil and the whole Rocket bench were on their feet yelling for more.

Which they promptly got. Justin tripled into the right field corner, sending Andy home. Brian singled up the middle, sending Justin home. Pete flied out deep to left, but the Rockets took the field leading 2–0.

6. Hit—and Run!

Andy mowed down the first batter in the second inning. The second hit a squibber down the first base line that Justin gloved a step from the bag. The third popped up to Luke in front of the plate. He squeezed it hard, and the Bombers were done.

But Pelsky was hot now, too. He struck out Jenny Carr on three pitches, and Michael Wong grounded out to short. He took Vicky Lopez to 0 and 2, got overconfident, and hit her!

The pitch wasn't thrown that hard, but Vicky turned right into it. With a cry of pain, she went down.

Luke was in the on-deck circle swinging his bat. He was the nearest to her and the first one there. She lay in the dirt, crying and holding her elbow. Her eyes were squeezed shut, her teeth were clenched,

and she kept squirming. She looked so little and so helpless. He didn't know what to do.

He touched her shoulder. "It's okay, Vicky."

Then Coach Channing was there and taking over. He picked Vicky up and helped her to the sideline. He brushed her off, asked how she was, examined her elbow. She winced a little but nodded she was all right.

"Good sport, Vicky," said the coach, and patted her on the back. Then she trotted down to first and jumped on the bag.

Luke stepped in and got ready. Time to get something started here, time to break out! He took a fastball down and in, but suddenly there was Vicky, running toward second base! He couldn't believe his eyes. He believed it even less when the Bombers' catcher easily threw her out. She didn't even slide, and it was the third out!

As Luke was strapping on his catcher's gear, Vicky passed him, going in to get her glove. He couldn't have been looking too pleased, because she stopped and said, "Sorry, Luke. I thought the steal sign was on."

Luke smiled up at her. He knew the steal sign—touch the belt buckle—would never have been on with two out, one on, and a two-nothing lead. He knew she'd taken off because she was freaked.

"Don't worry, Vick," he said. "We'll get 'em good next inning."

Top of the third. Andy seemed shaken by the incident with Vicky. He walked the first batter, went three and two on the second—and walked him! Then in stepped Steve Paretti, the Bombers' slugging right fielder. He was a big guy with close-cropped black hair. He knocked some dirt off his shoes with the end of the bat and got ready.

Andy looked as if he was going to panic. Quickly Luke called time and hustled to the mound.

"Take it easy, man. Just pitch this guy low and away. He'll golf the ball. He did before."

Andy nodded, pounded the ball into his glove, pulled at the peak of his cap. Luke patted him on the rump, walked back to the plate, and set the target.

Andy hesitated, his expression tight. Then he wound and fired—a fastball down the middle!

Luke could almost feel Paretti's swing, feel the thunder in the air as he snapped his wrists and the ball rocketed into left field over Brian's head at short. The runners took off, but Jenny charged the ball, fielded it quickly on the big hop, and pegged it in to Phil, who fired home to Luke from third.

It was too late to get the runner scoring, but Luke had anticipated that. He was standing in front of the plate, and as the ball arrived, he fired it back to Phil in time to get the runner sliding into third.

This turned out to be a crucial heads-up play. Steve Paretti was on second and the next batter walked, but then Andy settled down, got a grounder to third for the force and a pop-up to short for the third out. The Rockets came to bat still leading 2–1!

And Luke was coming up again—to finish what he'd barely started last inning. He was determined now, and he watched Pelsky carefully on every pitch. He ran the count to 2 and 0, then took a vicious cut at another one of those fat, looping change-ups and missed.

Shaken up, he concentrated very hard, took two more pitches, and walked. Not the hit he was looking for, but better than an easy out. He ran down to first instead of trotting, the way Coach Channing taught them to do, and when he saw that no one was covering second base, he kept on going and steamed in there standing up!

The Bombers looked shocked. They couldn't quite figure out what he was doing at second, but the few fans scattered around the bleachers knew and they began to cheer.

"Rah Rah Rockets!" Luke heard. *"Rah Rah Rockets!"*

Music to his ears. He took a two step lead, crouched on the balls of his feet, and scrambled back to second as Phil took Ball 1. Then, on the very next pitch, Phil lined a single to left, and Luke came around to score. There wasn't even a play at the plate. His heads-up baserunning had paid off, and the Rockets were ahead 3–1.

7. Fears and Cheers

In the top of the fourth, Andy fell apart. He walked the first batter; then Jim Bostwick, the Bomber third baseman, homered, and suddenly the score was tied! Coach Channing came out to talk, motioned for Justin to take over, and sent Andy to first.

Justin didn't have great speed as a pitcher, and he had the kind of slow delivery that tended to make infielders crazy. But he was very consistent, threw low strikes, and immediately got two ground balls and a line drive at Vicky for the third out.

Bottom of the fourth. Jenny squeezed out a walk, and Michael Wong moved her to second on a liner off Pelsky's glove. Two runners on, and Vicky Lopez coming up.

Vicky walked slowly to the batter's box. She stood as far from the plate as she could, and when the first pitch came, high and inside, she fell backward and sat down. Her father, Coach Lopez, came running out and called time. He hugged her, talked to her, tried to get her to calm down and stand in.

Nothing worked. She wouldn't anchor her back foot, stepped back with it on the next pitch, and flailed wildly at the ball. Finally, she struck out, swinging at a fastball nowhere near the strike zone.

Head down, trying to avoid the looks of the crowd, she started for the Rockets' bench. As Luke passed her on his way to the plate, he whispered, "It's okay, Vicky."

She smiled, but she hardly seemed to hear.

Luke continued on, but he might just as well not have bothered. Whether it was that funny smile, the effect of Vicky's performance, or something in the air, he would never know, but on the first pitch Pelsky threw, he bounced into a double play. He was so mad coming back from first he could hardly speak.

But Justin settled down nicely in the top of the fifth. He struck out the first batter he faced, and the second hit a slow roller to third. Phil had to charge it and make a good throw, but he beat the runner easily by two steps. Steve Paretti doubled to center for a scare, but the next batter popped up and the Bombers were gone.

And then things came together for the Rockets. Phil got on when his hard hit ground ball took a bad hop over the shortstop's head. He stole second on the next pitch, then moved to third on a passed ball. Andy crushed a deep fly to center, and Phil scored easily on the sacrifice. Luke gave him a big high-five when he reached the bench. Then Justin singled, and the Bombers yanked Pelsky.

They brought in a thin, dark lefty named Mike Charlton. He wore thick glasses and had a space between his front teeth. No one had ever heard of him, but Brian hit his first pitch to the fence in left center and Justin came all the way around to score in a tense play at the plate.

That was that, but the Bombers never really recovered from the play at the plate. They went down in order in the top of the sixth, and the Rockets had the victory 5–3.

There were high-fives and cheers, slaps on the back and digs in the ribs. Tired and sweaty, the dirt packed in under his fingernails, Luke joined in. But his own performance left him uncertain. He was pleased with his play in the field and his heads-up baserunning, but the fact that he was still not hitting gnawed away at him. Was everyone right? Was he really in a slump after all? He didn't want to admit that.

He had just finished packing up the catcher's gear when he noticed Vicky Lopez by the fence.

He had never seen anyone look more alone or sad. He couldn't tell if she was crying or not.

He had to do something. That was how he was. But what could he do?

He summoned up his courage.

"Vicky?"

"Yes, Luke."

"Meet me here tomorrow after school, and we'll work on your problem."

She turned to him now, her small cute features breaking into a grin below tear-filled black eyes.

"You really think you can help me?"

"Yes. Try not to be late. We'll need some time."

At that moment Coach Lopez appeared. It suddenly seemed funny to have offered to coach a coach's daughter, but when Vicky asked her father if it was okay about tomorrow, Coach Lopez said, "Sure, Luke. What a good idea."

Now all he had to do was round up Phil and Brian.

Phil was still hanging out by the backstop with a couple of the guys. He just shrugged and said "Why not?" Brian had already gone home, but when Luke called him that evening he agreed right away, then got in a little ribbing about the crush Luke must have on Vicky.

"Oh, come on, Brian," Luke said finally, "you're more of a pain than Jamey!"

8. Getting Together

Of course Luke was the first to arrive. He spent a few minutes fungoing the ball against the backstop. Then Vicky appeared, slowly, hesitantly, looking very small in that vast space that was the ballfield. Behind her, Phil and Brian arrived together, laughing, poking at each other, finishing some kind of private joke as they reached the diamond.

"Okay," Luke said when they had all assembled at home plate, "you know why we're here, and the first thing we're going to do is show Vicky how you get out of the way of a pitch that's too close."

Brian whispered something to Phil. They giggled.

"All right, guys," Luke said, "cut it out. I bet neither one of you knows the right way to fall."

Phil and Brian looked as if they'd each swallowed a baseball. They shook their heads no.

"My dad taught me this," Luke said. He took a bat, stepped into the batter's box, and got into his stance. "When the pitch comes in, you keep turning your body away from it, lower your head, and fall down. That way you can only get hit in the butt and the back of your legs. It doesn't hurt so much that way."

He picked himself up. "Dad said you don't ever want to turn into the pitch. That's how you get clobbered. Vicky, you try."

She did. Then she did it again.

"See," Luke said, "easy. Knowing how not to get hurt is the first step toward not being afraid. Phil, Brian, you're next. Vicky's gonna watch you to see you do it right."

They did.

"Bravo," Luke said. "Okay, now I've got another drill my dad showed me. Take a bat and lock it in your arms behind your back. Get into your batting stance, step forward with your front foot, and grind your back foot into the ground like you were squashing a bug."

Luke had brought three bats. Everyone grabbed one and did it.

"How does that feel?" Luke asked.

"Feels good," Vicky said. "I like the rhythm."

"That's the way you bring your legs and body into your swing. It should feel natural and rhythmic, just like Vicky said. You don't ever step back with your back foot. That's bailing out. Okay, try it some more times and then I've got something else."

They kept on stepping and grinding, stepping and grinding.

"Hey," Phil said finally, "I think I killed the bug."

"Good," said Luke. "Vicky, I want you in the batter's box, Brian pitching, Phil in the field. I'll be in my usual place, you know where."

Everyone did as Luke instructed, but as Vicky stepped into the box, Luke lined up two bats parallel behind her legs.

"I want you to stand in there," Luke

said. "Brian's going to pitch to you. He'll start out pretty slow, then he'll get faster, but I don't want you to swing. Just watch the ball. Track it all the way from Brian's hand across the plate, and don't—whatever happens—step back. If you do, you'll break your leg on one of these bats."

Vicky looked a little nervous, but she stepped in, took a few swings with her bat, faced Brian.

"Looking good," Luke said. "Now remember to watch the ball."

Brian went into his windup and threw, nice and easy, right over the plate. Vicky tracked the ball into Luke's mitt.

"Good going," Luke said. "Keep it up."

Again Brian wound and threw, and again Vicky stood watching. Again and again the ball thwacked into Luke's mitt, but the first time Brian threw a fastball, Vicky stumbled backward, fell over the bats, and sat down.

Luke helped her up. "Are you okay?"

Vicky nodded.

"Remember, you know how not to get hurt. You know how you've got to con-

56

centrate. Now I want you to get back in there, *knowing* you won't be afraid."

Vicky did, and Brian threw some more. Vicky never flinched. She tracked the ball every single time.

"All *right*," Luke said finally. "Now I want you to practice bunting."

"Bunting?" Vicky said.

"Yes, bunting. Great for eye and hand coordination. Great for concentration and timing."

He didn't tell her that when you squared around to bunt, there was no way you could bail out, but that was okay. She probably realized what he was up to anyway.

Vicky knew the fundamentals, knew how to square around facing the pitcher and how to move her hands up so she could bunt the ball off the fat part of the bat. Luke had her get into the batter's box, and then he had Brian move forward from the mound and pitch her slow and easy, then a little faster in a kind of modified pepper drill until she got the hang of it. In no time she was bunting the ball back to the mound, then down the third and first base lines. She even seemed to be liking it.

After a while, Luke said, "Okay, let's all of us play pepper."

They fanned into the outfield, Vicky with the bat and Phil, Luke, and Brian pitching to her at half speed, each one fielding the ball as she bunted it back to them and someone different throwing each time. Soon she was hitting every pitch.

"Go, Vicky!" Luke said, and then he brought her back into the plate and had Brian pitch to her as if they were in a game.

First he had her bunt. Then he said, "Hit the ball! You're mad at it. Go for it!"

And Vicky did. She kept her cool, but she began swinging at pitches she thought she could hit. She didn't bail out, she didn't look scared, and she began to meet the ball. Who would have believed she was the same kid who wouldn't take an inside pitch a little while ago?

Crouching behind the plate, watching

Phil chase grounders and fly balls around the field, Luke smiled to himself. You did good, kid, he thought, and then, as if from nowhere, a light went on in his head. If Vicky could get her timing back by bunting, why couldn't he? If he could help her, why couldn't he help himself?

He let Brian hurl a few more. Then he stood up and called time. "Vicky, you're doing great. Now I'd like you all to help me out of my slump."

Everyone looked stunned.

"So you're finally admitting it?" Brian said.

"Yes," Luke said. "I thought I had it licked, but I don't. I need you guys to help. Will you do it?"

"Of course," said Phil.

"You bet," said Brian.

"I'll help, too," said Vicky. "Anything you want, Luke."

"Thanks, everyone, and Phil, Brian, I'm sorry I was so mean to you before. It wasn't very nice of me."

"Hey," said Brian, slapping hands with Luke, "it's okay. We've all been there. We know how you felt."

"Yeah," said Phil, "we're your friends. We just want you to start clobbering the ball again."

Luke put his arms around them both. "Great. Let's start."

Vicky moved out into the field, Brian took over as catcher, and Phil moved in to throw some pitches, even though he wasn't really a pitcher at all.

"Better this way for a while," Luke said. "Don't want Brian ruining his arm."

And now it was Luke up at bat, Luke doing the bunting drill, and at first he was missing the ball or not making good contact, but he stood in there and he started to get better, started to get good wood, started to hit! He could feel his confidence building, could feel himself seeing the ball and meeting it, and when he got Brian back on the mound, got him firing his good stuff, he was hitting that, too.

It had worked for Vicky. It was working for him, too!

9. Home Free

At Friday's practice Vicky kept on looking better. She would never be a big hitter, but she was making contact and smacking some solid line drives.

As she finished her licks, Luke glanced up from his crouch. "Guess we won't need those extra bats now."

Vicky smiled. "Thanks, Luke."

He smiled back. He was sure he had done well, and not just for Vicky but for himself. He was swinging the bat much better today. He was meeting the ball and getting some hits. He *had* to be ready for tomorrow's game.

It was at home against the Hurricanes. Josh Rubin was pitching. Adam Spinelli was subbing for Michael Wong in center field, and Andy McClellan was in left for Jennifer Carr. When Luke arrived at the park with his dad, the stands were already filled with spectators. Everyone was cheering wildly. The Hurricanes were supposed to be tough!

At first Josh seemed too aware of that. He was very jittery, and he walked the first two batters. Luke went out to settle him down, but the next pitch he threw was wild and the runners advanced to second and third.

"Boo!" yelled a few of the fans, and that didn't help matters, especially since Blair Tolan, the Hurricanes' dangerous number three hitter, was at bat.

He crowded the plate and shook off a couple of pitches, then let Josh burn a fastball by him on the inside corner for a strike. Clearly he was not going to let that happen again. At 2 and 1, he reached over and smacked a change-up, low and outside, into the right field corner for a double. Both runs scored, and already things looked bleak.

Coach Channing and Luke headed for the mound, but when they got there, Josh faced them down. Cool and confident, his small frame ramrod straight, he pounded the ball into his glove.

"I'm all right," he said. "I can do it."

Coach Channing stood blinking for a moment. "Go for it, Josh," he said, and left, motioning for Luke to follow.

Josh was as good as his word. He got the cleanup hitter on a weak ground out to Brian at short. Then he came on even stronger and struck out the next two batters with his weird sidearm motion.

"Good stuff, Josh!" Luke said, but he didn't have long to think about it. As usual, he was leading off in the bottom of the first.

But he felt good again, confident and full of beans despite those two runs scored. The Hurricane pitcher was a tall, silent fastballer named Todd Stallworthy, and as he reared and fired, Luke squared around and bunted the first pitch down the third base line!

It wasn't a terrific bunt, but Stallworthy and the Hurricanes' third baseman were taken so completely by surprise Luke beat it out for a hit. Standing on first, looking over at the bench, he saw

Coach Channing smiling and shaking his head.

Then he checked Coach Carr at third. The steal sign was on! He took off on the next pitch, sliding in safe under the tag. "Come on, Rockets!" he heard the crowd. "Come on, *Phil!*"

Phil Hubbard took a fastball and popped up on a change, but Luke went to third on Andy McClellan's hard grounder that the second baseman misplayed into center field. He took a big lead and was so distracting dancing back and forth that Stallworthy uncorked a wild pitch. Luke came in to score, Andy moved to second, Justin doubled him home, and the score was tied 2–2!

Things stayed that way for two more innings. Josh had become dazzling, throwing sidearm heat and confusing the hitters. Stallworthy threw nothing but strikes. It was just that no one seemed able to hit them.

But for Luke there was a great moment in the bottom of the second. It was when Vicky Lopez came up to bat for the first time. She looked calm and determined. She anchored her back foot and stood tall against the giant Stallworthy. She strode into the first pitch and missed. She strode into the second pitch and looped a high fly ball into center field. It was easily caught for the out, but when she got back to the bench, Luke hugged her. Both of them knew what that meant.

Though it didn't make him feel any better when he led off the bottom of the third and lined out to the shortstop. Well, at least he got a piece of it, but in the top of the fourth, the Hurricanes squeezed in another run, scratching out a single after two walks. Then they scored again when Adam Spinelli dropped a fly ball in center field.

Luke was the first to cheer up Adam when he walked dejectedly off the field at the end of the inning. He poked him on the arm and told him he was okay, that everyone goofed up once in a while. Adam seemed really pleased. He looked more like himself when he reached the bench.

The kindness paid off almost at once. After Justin struck out, Brian walked and Pete Wyshansky doubled him to third. Then Adam got up and promptly punched a single to right that scored both runs and tied the game at 4.

A little restored confidence went a long way, but Josh grounded out to third and on the first inside fastball Stallworthy threw her, Vicky fell backward and sat down. Uh oh, thought Luke, but she got up, brushed herself off, and slammed the next pitch right at the left fielder. It was a good, solid shot that could have been for extra bases. Luke knew she was back on track now!

Top of the fifth. Josh got a strikeout and a fly ball. Then Blair Tolan hit a solo home run, and the Hurricanes led 5–4.

Josh still had some good stuff, but it was clear he was tiring. Coach Channing brought in Justin, who was always reliable, even in the clutch.

Justin walked one batter, then set down two as the runner who had walked moved over to third on a ground ball. The Rocket infield was ready for any sort of ground ball or pop-up, but at that point there was the kind of freak play no one could ever explain.

Justin got the grounder, but it was down the line at third. Phil backhanded the ball and threw, but for some reason he forgot that little Josh was now playing first, not big Justin. The throw sailed over Josh's head, the run scored, and it was 6–4 Hurricanes!

Justin struck out the next batter, but in the bottom of the inning, the Rockets went down one-two-three. Luke lined out again, this time to third.

Things did not look good, but the Hurricanes failed to score in the top of the sixth. As the Rockets came up for their last licks, they were still trailing 6–4.

Stallworthy was going strong, but Brian led off with a single to right and Pete followed with one to left, sending Brian to third.

The crowd came alive. *"Rah Rah Rockets! Rah Rah Rockets!"*

The Hurricane coach hurried to the mound, stood there for a moment with his hands in his hip pockets, liked what he heard, and left. Then Adam Spinelli slammed a sacrifice fly to center, and speedy Brian hustled home.

The score was now 6–5.

Pete had tagged up and gone to second on the sacrifice, but Josh now grounded out to short, leaving Pete where he was. With two out and hope fading, Vicky Lopez came to the plate.

Everyone on the Rockets' bench seemed restless. Andy McClellan coughed into his fist. But standing in the on-deck circle, Luke knew Vicky would come through.

She stood in and fouled off a mean Stallworthy fastball. On the very next pitch she slapped a base hit up the middle! When the center fielder was slow picking up the ball, Pete scored easily from third.

Everyone on the Rockets' bench was standing and yelling as Luke stepped into the batter's box.

He was proud of Vicky, and he was sure of himself. He worked the count to 2 and 1, 2 and 2, 3 and 2, and then he got his pitch, a fastball down and away. He stepped into it, the way he always did, and he felt that delicious, chilling

sensation as bat met ball. He knew at once that it was solid and for extra bases to left, and he took off, roaring into second as Vicky reached third!

But the score was still 6–6, and there were still two out.

The crowd grew quiet. Phil Hubbard came to the plate. He took a called strike and a ball. He took another strike, and then he swung and jerked a little looper over the first baseman's head.

Vicky raced for home. The right fielder scooped up the ball and threw. Vicky heard the thwack in the catcher's mitt. She hit the dirt and slid around his tag with the winning run!

"Safe!" yelled the umpire.

Immediately the Rockets' bench surrounded her, but Luke fought his way through and hugged her. "We did it!" they shouted over and over. "We did it!"

And then the rest of the Rockets were on top of them. Hugs, high-fives, jumping up and down.

"We knew you'd break out of your slump!" Michael Wong yelled at Luke.

"We knew you'd get tough again!" Andy McClellan yelled at Vicky.

"It was Luke who made the difference," Vicky said.

"Vicky, Phil, and Brian helped me," Luke said.

"All of us together," said Brian.

"Yeah, all of us together," said Luke.